THE
KNOW-NOTHINGS
TALK TURKEY

story by Michele Sobel Spirn
pictures by R. W. Alley

HarperCollins*Publishers*

For my sister, Jill Gross, another bedtime story;
for Josh, the legal Know-It-All;
and for Steve, my first and best reader

—M.S.S.

With thanks to Michele for Boris, Norris, Morris, and Doris
(and Floris)

—R.W.A.

HarperCollins®, 📖®, and I Can Read Book® are trademarks of HarperCollins Publishers Inc.

The Know-Nothings Talk Turkey
Text copyright © 2000 by Michele Sobel Spirn
Illustrations copyright © 2000 by R. W. Alley
Printed in the U.S.A. All rights reserved.
www.harperchildrens.com

Library of Congress Cataloging-in-Publication Data
Spirn, Michele.
    The Know-Nothings talk turkey / by Michele Sobel Spirn ; pictures by R. W. Alley.
    p.   cm.
    Summary: Four friends celebrate Thanksgiving in their own silly way.
    ISBN 0-06-028183-9. — ISBN 0-06-028184-7 (lib. bdg.)
    [1. Thanksgiving Day—Fiction.   2. Turkeys—Fiction.   3. Friendship—Fiction.
4. Humorous stories.]   I. Alley, R. W. (Robert W.), ill.   II. Title.
PZ7.S757Kp   2000   99-10608
[E]—dc21   CIP
                                                                                        AC

2   3   4   5   6   7   8   9   10
❖

CONTENTS

A SPECIAL DAY

Boris, Morris, Doris, and Norris

were four good friends called

the Know-Nothings.

They didn't know much,

but they knew they liked each other.

"Today is a special day," said Doris.

"It is Thanksgiving."

6

"Thanksgiving, hooray!"

cried Norris.

"I must buy a tree and get gifts

for you and Boris and Morris."

"That's not Thanksgiving,"
said Doris. "That's Christmas."

"I must color the eggs," said Boris.

"That's Easter," said Doris.

"I will cut red paper hearts
for all of us," said Morris.
"That's Valentine's Day,"
said Doris.
"Today is Thanksgiving.
I read about it in a book.
It said Thanksgiving is about turkeys
and being thankful."

9

"It doesn't sound like much fun,"
said Norris.

"It will be lots of fun," Doris said.

"We can have a Thanksgiving dinner."

"Dinner! That sounds like fun,"
said Norris.

Doris said, "The book says
there is a parade, too."

"I love parades!" said Boris.

"We can have a parade
to honor the Pilgrims,"
said Doris.
"Who are the Pilgrims?"
Morris asked.

"They had the first Thanksgiving,"
Doris said. "They sailed
from Europe to America in a big boat
that landed on a rock
called Plymouth."

"I have a boat," said Morris.

"My rock does not have a name,"

said Norris, "but it would like

to be in the parade."

"Boris and I can carry the turkey
in the parade," said Doris.

"What?" asked Boris.

"We have to serve turkey
for Thanksgiving," said Doris.

"Turkey! That is a very big country.
We can't do that!" said Morris.

"No," said Doris.

"We serve one turkey, a bird."

"Where do we get a turkey?"

asked Morris.

"The book says they are wild

and live in the woods,"

said Doris.

"Let's go!" said Boris.

So off they went to get a turkey

for Thanksgiving.

CALLING ALL TURKEYS

"I don't see any turkeys,"
said Morris.
"Maybe we should call one,"
Boris said.
"We don't know
the phone number,"
said Morris.

"I will try calling one
without a phone," said Norris.
"Gobble, gobble, gobble."

"Norris, you are so clever,"
said Doris. "You can talk turkey."

The Know-Nothings waited,

but no turkeys came.

21

"I know," said Boris.

"These turkeys are wild.

We must be wild, too.

Then they will come."

"I will be wild," said Morris.

"I will hop like a wild rabbit."

"I will kick like a wild horse,"
said Norris.

"I will jump like a wild frog,"
said Boris.

24

"I will flap my arms
like a wild bird," said Doris.
The Know-Nothings hopped
and kicked and jumped and flapped
until they came to a farm.

"Look!" cried Doris. "Turkeys!

They were here all the time."

"No wonder they didn't come.
They were too far away to hear us,"
said Norris.

"Can I help you?" the farmer asked.

Boris said, "We would like

to serve a turkey for Thanksgiving."

"Of course," said the farmer.

"We would like a good one,"

Doris said.

"You can bring it back

if it's not good," said the farmer.

"Thank you," said Doris.

"We will carry him in our parade."

"When is your parade?"

asked the farmer.

"Now," said Doris.

Morris carried the boat.

Norris held the rock.

Boris and Doris carried the turkey.

"This turkey is hard to hold,"
Boris said.

"I think he wants to go home.

Maybe he misses his friends."

"Turkey, you will have a good time
with us," said Doris.
"And if you do not want to stay,
we will bring you back tomorrow."

"Let's make him feel at home,"

said Morris. "Let's be wild."

So the Know-Nothings hopped,

kicked, jumped, flapped,

and gobbled all the way home.

SERVING THE WILD TURKEY

The Know-Nothings got ready

for Thanksgiving dinner.

Doris made string beans.

Boris mashed potatoes.

Morris put dressing on the salad.

Norris cooked squash.

"Yum, yum," said Boris.

"Let's eat."

"Not yet," said Doris.

"First we have to serve the turkey."

Norris tried to get the turkey

to sit down.

Morris and Boris had to help him.

"Now, turkey, what can I serve you?"

asked Doris.

The turkey said, "Gobble."

"The turkey wants some salad,"

said Morris.

"Morris, you are so clever!"

said Doris.

"You have learned to talk turkey, too."

"Ouch! I think the turkey

would rather eat me,"

Norris said.

"I'll give him some string beans,"

said Boris.

The turkey dropped the string beans

on the floor.

"The farmer promised us a good turkey,
but this turkey is rude!"
Doris said.
"The turkey is wilder than we are,"
said Norris.

"We tried to serve the turkey,"

said Doris.

"Now we should tell

what we are thankful for."

"I am thankful you told us

about Thanksgiving," said Morris.

"I am thankful

I don't have to be wild anymore,"

said Norris.

"I am thankful we can take

the turkey back tomorrow,"

said Boris.

"I am thankful for good friends,"
said Doris.

The turkey said, "Gobble."

"He is thankful, too!"

said Doris. "Just like us."

And so the Know-Nothings
ate their Thanksgiving dinner
and let the turkey serve himself.